GROSSET & DUNLAP
Published by the Penguin Group
Penguin Group (USA) Inc., 375 Hudson Street, New York, New York 10014, USA
Penguin Group (Canada), 90 Eglinton Avenue East, Suite 700,
Toronto, Ontario M4P 2Y3, Canada
(a division of Pearson Penguin Canada Inc.)
Penguin Books Ltd., 80 Strand, London WC2R 0RL, England
Penguin Group Ireland, 25 St. Stephen's Green, Dublin 2, Ireland
(a division of Penguin Books Ltd.)
Penguin Group (Australia), 250 Camberwell Road, Camberwell, Victoria 3124, Australia
(a division of Pearson Australia Group Pty. Ltd.)
Penguin Books India Pvt. Ltd., 11 Community Centre, Panchsheel Park,
New Delhi—110 017, India
Penguin Group (NZ), 67 Apollo Drive, Rosedale, North Shore 0632, New Zealand
(a division of Pearson New Zealand Ltd.)
Penguin Books (South Africa) (Pty.) Ltd., 24 Sturdee Avenue,
Rosebank, Johannesburg 2196, South Africa

Penguin Books Ltd., Registered Offices:
80 Strand, London WC2R 0RL, England

Illustrated by Andrew Grey and Stuart Trotter. Text by Jude Exley.

ISBN 978-0-448-45560-0   10 9 8 7 6 5 4 3 2 1

Tigger's Tales

Grosset & Dunlap
An Imprint of Penguin Group (USA) Inc.

Tigger Comes to the Forest

One night Pooh woke up suddenly when he thought he heard somebody trying to get into his honey cupboard. He got out of bed, but no one was there— just a strange noise. There were lots of noises in the Forest, but this was different.

It wasn't a growl

or a purr

or a squeak

or a neigh,

like Piglet or Eeyore might make. It was a

worrdworrdworrdworrdworrd.

Pooh decided to ask the strange animal making that noise not to do it again. So he opened his front door and said, "Hello."

The strange animal introduced himself as Tigger. Pooh had never seen a Tigger before, but he was very pleased to hear that he was a friend of Christopher Robin's, and invited him in.

"Do Tiggers like honey?" asked Pooh.

"Tiggers like everything," said Tigger happily. And they both went to sleep.

The next morning, Pooh woke up to see Tigger looking at himself in the mirror.

"I thought I was the only one," said Tigger, "but I've just met someone like me!"

Then suddenly Tigger jumped at Pooh's tablecloth. With a loud

worrdworrdworrdworrdworrd,

he pulled it off the table and rolled across the room with it.

"Did I win?" Tigger asked cheerfully.

"That's my tablecloth," replied Pooh, putting the cloth and two pots of honey on the table.

They both sat down to breakfast, and Tigger
helped himself to a large mouthful of honey,
making exploring movements with his tongue . . .
and "what-is-this" noises . . .
and then he said,
"Tiggers don't like honey."
"I thought they liked everything," said
Pooh, trying to sound disappointed, but actually
feeling very pleased—particularly when Tigger
said that they liked everything except honey.

Pooh took Tigger to Piglet's house. Piglet had never seen a Tigger before and he was a little bit scared. But Pooh explained that Tigger would like some haycorns for breakfast, and Piglet said, "Help yourself."

When Tigger had a mouthful of haycorns, he said, "Ee-ers o i a-ors." Then, "Skoos ee," before saying firmly, "Tiggers don't like haycorns."

Piglet was rather glad and asked if he would like thistles instead, and Tigger said that was what he liked best.

Pooh, Piglet, and Tigger went to the part of the Forest where Eeyore lived. Eeyore was a little unsure of Tigger at first, and asked what he was and when he was going. But when Pooh explained that Tigger was a friend of Christopher Robin's who wanted some thistles for breakfast, Eeyore showed him to a very thistly-looking patch of thistles.

Tigger wasn't sure that these really were the thistles that Tiggers like best, but he took a large, crunchy mouthful.

"Ow! Hot!" said Tigger, putting his paw in his mouth and shaking his head to get the prickles out.

Eeyore thought that Tigger had eaten a bee, but Tigger, running around in circles with his tongue hanging out, explained that Tiggers don't like thistles.

Pooh was very confused. Tiggers didn't like honey, haycorns, or thistles. Maybe Christopher Robin could help. So they went to find Christopher Robin, with Tigger bouncing in front of them, turning around every now and then to check that this was the right way.

Soon Tigger saw Christopher Robin and rushed up to him.

"Oh, there you are, Tigger!" said Christopher Robin.

Pooh asked Christopher Robin what Tiggers like to eat for breakfast, but he didn't know, either. He thought Kanga would be able to help. So they all went to Kanga's house.

Pooh was very pleased to find some **condensed milk** in Kanga's cupboard. But Tigger put his nose into this and his paw into that, and he still couldn't find anything that Tiggers like.

Then they saw Kanga trying to give Roo his Strengthening Medicine. Roo was trying his best not to have it, when Tigger suddenly put out his tongue, and the Extract of Malt medicine went straight into Tigger's mouth.

"Tigger, dear!" said Kanga.

"He's taken my medicine!" sang Roo happily.

Then Tigger closed his eyes, moved his tongue around and around, and with a happy smile on his face said, "So that's what Tiggers like!"

Everyone was very happy to know, finally, what Tiggers like. And from then on, it was decided that Tigger would live at Kanga's house, so he could eat Extract of Malt for breakfast, dinner, and tea. And sometimes as Strengthening Medicine, too.

A few days later, Kanga was beginning to realize that there were times when a bouncy animal like Tigger shouldn't be in the house. So she sent Tigger and Roo out to have a nice, long morning in the Forest, not getting into mischief.

Tigger was telling Roo about all the things Tiggers can do. Roo was very excited to learn that climbing trees is what Tiggers do best.

So Roo sat on Tigger's back, and Tigger began to climb a very tall tree. It was going well until . . .

SNAP!!!

The branch he was standing on started to break . . .
and Tigger had to climb quickly onto the one
above it. Roo was having lots of fun, and couldn't
wait to go higher. But Tigger told him that he
didn't want to go any higher, and that his tail got
in the way if he tried to climb down.

Just then, Pooh and Piglet came along.

"Hallo, Roo," called Piglet. "What are you doing?"

"We can't get down!" cried Roo. "Isn't it fun? Tigger and I are living in a tree, just like Owl."

Pooh and Piglet didn't know how to get them down, either. Luckily, Christopher Robin came strolling along, and decided that he would take off his tunic so they could hold it out under the tree for Roo and Tigger to jump into.

Roo was wildly excited, and he jumped straight into the tunic, bouncing back up into the air when he landed, and saying, "Ooh, lovely!" for a while.

Tigger was less sure. He was holding onto the branch nervously until suddenly, with a crash and a tearing noise, Tigger flew through the air and landed in a heap with everyone on the ground. They all picked themselves up, and Tigger bounced happily away with little Roo.

Tigger Gets Unbounced

After a while, some of the animals in the Forest began to get annoyed by Tigger's bounciness.

One sunny day, Rabbit was talking to Pooh and Piglet about teaching Tigger a lesson. Piglet agreed that however much you liked Tigger, it was a very good idea to think of a way to unbounce him. But Piglet wasn't sure how they should do it. And Pooh was humming to himself, so it was left to Rabbit to come up with an idea.

Rabbit decided that they would take Tigger exploring to the **North Pole** and lose him there, so that by the time he found his way home, he would be a very different Tigger altogether. Pooh was glad that they were going to the North Pole, as Tigger would see the sign that said Pooh had found it, and then Tigger would know what sort of bear Pooh was.

The next morning, it was cold and misty. Piglet was **worried** about how miserable it would be for Tigger to be lost on a day like this. But Rabbit thought that it was the perfect weather, as when Tigger **bounced** out of sight, they could hide and he wouldn't be able to see them.

"Not never?" said Piglet worriedly.

"Well, not until we find him again," said Rabbit.

At Kanga's house, Tigger and Roo were very pleased to see their friends and very excited at the thought of an adventure. But Rabbit didn't think Tigger's good friend Roo should come along.

"He was coughing earlier," Rabbit told Kanga.

"It was just a biscuit cough," said Roo.

"Oh, Roo dear," said Kanga. "You can go another day." And it was decided that Roo would stay at home.

So, off they
went. Pooh, Rabbit,
and Piglet walked
together. Tigger
ran around them in
circles, squares,
and, when the
bushes got prickly,

up and down in front of them. He kept bouncing
into Rabbit and then disappearing into the mist.

Rabbit decided that now was the right time. He
jumped into a gap beside the path, and Pooh and Piglet
followed him.

The Forest was silent. Then they heard Tigger say,
"Hello?"

They all waited silently until they heard Tigger
wander off. Piglet felt very brave. When they were sure
Tigger had left, and they were all beginning to get a bit
scared in the dark gap, they hurried off, with Rabbit
leading the way home.

"Why are we going this way?" asked Pooh.

"I thought we went right," said Piglet nervously.

But Rabbit was sure he knew the way, and half an hour later, he kept saying,

"Here we are"
and "No, we're not."

And then,

"It's lucky I know the Forest so well,
or we might get lost."

Tigger waited for the others to catch up to
him, but when he got tired of waiting, he went
home. Kanga was waiting for him with his
Strengthening Medicine.

Just as they finished dinner, Christopher Robin
arrived. He soon realized that
Pooh, Piglet, and Rabbit
were lost in the Forest.

"Tiggers never get
lost," whispered
Tigger to Roo.

Christopher
Robin asked
Tigger to help him
find them, and off
they went.

Rabbit, Pooh, and Piglet were having a rest in a
sandpit that they seemed to keep ending up in. Pooh
was sure that his honey-pots were calling him,
but he couldn't hear them because Rabbit kept talking.
So Pooh persuaded Rabbit to set off again by himself.
Rabbit walked into the mist, and after twenty minutes,
Pooh and Piglet walked off together.

Just when Pooh and Piglet began to know where they were, out of the mist came Christopher Robin.

"Oh, there you are," he said carelessly, trying to pretend that he wasn't worried. "Tigger will find Rabbit. He's sort of looking for you all."

"We are just going home for a little something," said Pooh, and Christopher Robin decided to go home with them.

Meanwhile, Tigger was bouncing around the Forest, making loud, yapping noises, looking for Rabbit.

At last, a very small and sorry Rabbit heard him. Rabbit rushed to the noise to discover that it was a Friendly Tigger, who bounced in just the way a Tigger should bounce.

"Oh, Tigger. I am very glad to see you," Rabbit cried happily. And off they went home together.